Gorgonzola Zombies in the Park

GORGONZOLA ZOMBIES in the PARK

by **Elizabeth Levy**
illustrated by **George Ulrich**

HarperCollins*Publishers*

Library of Congress Cataloging-in-Publication Data
Levy, Elizabeth.
   Gorgonzola zombies in the park / Elizabeth Levy ; illustrated by George
Ulrich.
     p.   cm.
   Summary: Sam and Robert make up a story about a Gorgonzola Zombie
to scare their cousin Mabel, but strange and scary events convince all three
that there really is a zombie haunting Central Park.
   ISBN 0-06-021461-9. — ISBN 0-06-021460-0 (lib. bdg.)
   [1. Cousins—Fiction.   2. Monsters—Fiction.   3. Central Park (New
York, N.Y.)—Fiction.   4. New York (N.Y.)—Fiction]   I. Ulrich, George, ill.
II. Title.
PZ7.L5827Go   1993   92-11353
[Fic]—dc20   CIP
                                               AC

*To all the joy I've found in Central Park
and the people who work to preserve it*

Contents

1

Mabel, The Orange Peel

"Her mom *said* she'd be easy to spot," said Mrs. Bamford, waving to her niece Mabel as she came off the airplane. This was Mabel's first trip to New York City. Sam and Robert Bamford hadn't seen their cousin Mabel from San Francisco in three years. Sam and Robert could have happily waited another three years.

"The last time we saw Mabel, she called me weird eyes because I wear glasses," Sam muttered. "Then she said that my sneezes sounded like honks."

"She told me my ears stuck out like Dumbo's," said Robert. "She was only five then. Imagine what she's like now."

"Over here, Mabel." Mrs. Bamford waved again. Mabel was nothing if not color coordinated. She had on an orange short pleated skirt, an orange-and-white polka-dotted blouse with matching socks, and an orange head-band with glitter stars on it. Mrs. Bamford rushed up and gave Mabel a kiss.

"She looks like an orange peel," whispered Robert to Sam.

Mrs. Bamford brought Mabel over to her two sons. "Mabel, you remember Sam and Robert. They haven't seen you since you were just a little girl."

"I'm very grown up now," said Mabel. She was eyeing Sam and Robert suspiciously. "Your ears still stick out, Robert," she said. "And Sam, I see your honker's gotten bigger so you can keep your glasses on."

Mrs. Bamford laughed nervously. "I think it's just jet lag," she whispered to her boys. They walked down the corridor of the airport to get Mabel's luggage.

"She's definitely changed for the worse," whispered Robert. "And she wasn't any treat to begin with."

When they got to the baggage-claim area, Mrs. Bamford took Mabel's claim checks and told her to stay with Sam and Robert.

"How old are you now, Robert?" Mabel asked.

"Seven and three quarters," said Robert.

"I'm eight," said Mabel. "I'm older. My birthday was last week."

"Yeah, but you're from San Francisco," said Robert. "And we're on the East Coast, so our birthdays are sooner."

Mabel looked confused.

Sam winked at Robert. Sam understood what Robert was trying to do to Mabel. He thought he'd help him out. "Look, Mabel, what time is it now in San Francisco?"

Mabel looked at her watch, which Robert noticed had an orange wristband. "It's two o'clock," she said. "We're three hours behind New York."

Sam loved to do math in his head. "You were born in San Francisco. For eight years you've been losing three hours a day. Three goes into twenty-four—eight—so it's one eighth of the time you've been alive. You lost a year. You're just seven years old, New York time."

"We should give her leap year," said Robert seriously.

Sam nodded. "That's only fair."

Mabel looked confused and more than a little angry. "Yeah," said Mabel, "leap year

4

comes once every four years, so I get two extra days on my side."

"Like Sam said," admitted Robert, "that's fair."

"Thanks," said Mabel.

"But you are still my *younger* cousin," said Robert.

"Yeah," said Sam. "You're our youngest cousin."

Mabel swallowed hard, but she didn't deny that she was younger.

Robert and Sam gave each other a high five behind her back.

Mrs. Bamford came back with Mabel's luggage. It was orange. Sam and Robert helped their mom carry it to the taxi stand.

"Do you smell something weird?" whispered Robert.

"Yeah, it's Mabel," said Sam. "Mabel, the orange peel."

You Do, Voodoo

Mabel stayed very quiet in the taxi ride home from the airport. Mrs. Bamford looked at Robert and Sam suspiciously. "Mabel, are you all right?" she asked.

"Oh, yes," said Mabel, sitting between Sam and Robert. She was still trying to figure out how she had lost a year in a six-hour plane trip.

"My younger cousin's from San Francisco," Robert explained to the taxi driver. "It's a little city in California."

"I've heard of San Francisco," said the taxi driver. "It's supposed to be *magnifique*." The taxi driver was from Haiti, and he spoke English with a French accent.

"What could be prettier than this?" said Mrs. Bamford as they drove over the Triborough Bridge. There were sailboats and tugboats on

the East River. The sun sparkled off the water.

"It looks a little like the Golden Gate Bridge," said Mabel, "only not as pretty."

They got stuck in traffic coming off the bridge. The taxi driver fumed. "If we don't move, we can't go through Central Park," he said.

"I heard the park is very dangerous," said Mabel.

"Not if you know what you're doing," said Robert.

"I play music in the park," said the cab driver. "The city needs my playing. It is good voodoo."

"Voodoo," whispered Robert. "That's scary."

"No, no," said the driver. "Voodoo is spirit. You see, everything you do—every mood you're in—it can change the universe. You do something bad—you're mean to somebody—don't tip the cab driver—it comes back to haunt you. So I do what I can to keep my tiny part of the universe okay. I play my music."

"I knew New York was a creepy place," said Mabel. "Voodoo in the park." She shivered.

Robert leaned forward so that he could read the cab driver's identification. Robert loved to listen to music in the park. And he liked the idea of a good kind of voodoo.

"Alphonse DeLemeuil," Robert read out loud, struggling with the pronunciation. There was a picture of Mr. DeLemeuil. "Mr. DeLemeuil, what instrument do you play?"

"Call me Alphonse. I play the conga drums. The spirits like drums." He began demonstrating by banging away on the steering wheel with his right hand. Mabel closed her eyes as they sped past a parked delivery truck with just inches to spare.

"What about zombies?" asked Sam. "Doesn't voodoo have to do with zombies?"

"*Absolument*," said Alphonse. "The zombies, they are the living dead. They are spirits who did something wrong and they cannot die. They make life miserable for the rest of us."

"I think that's enough talk about voodoo," said Mrs. Bamford firmly.

At the edge of Harlem, they turned into the park. Even though it was a weekday, runners and bicyclists competed for space in the left-hand lane. The trees and the flowers were beautiful, but crumpled-up newspapers flew in the breeze.

"The garbage, it drives me crazy," said Alphonse.

"Me too," said Mrs. Bamford.

"I heard New York's very scary and smelly," said Mabel. "Kind of like you, Robert," she whispered, low enough to keep Mrs. Bamford from hearing her. Mabel's spirits were reviving.

Robert felt like bopping her on the nose.

Finally, they pulled up in front of the Bamfords' apartment building. Ray McKenna, the new superintendent, was sweeping up the sidewalk. Ray loved to see the street clean. Mrs. Bamford called him the Warrior Broom of West 74th Street. He patrolled the block, picking up garbage, reminding everyone to use the trash barrels.

"Hi, Ray," said Robert. "This is my cousin Mabel, my *younger* cousin Mabel. Mabel, you'd better not drop any garbage on the street. Ray will trash you." Ray smiled at Mabel. Mabel thought it was a scary smile.

Alphonse, the taxi driver, got Mabel's luggage out of the trunk. "Something smells familiar," he said as he put the suitcase down.

"Something stinks," said Ray with a frown.

"I'll take that bag," said Mabel. "It's got a present for you all."

"A stinky present?" asked Sam.

Mrs. Bamford gave him a warning look.

"Have a good visit," said Alphonse. "Come visit me in the park. Every day after I finish work, I make music in the park right near here."

"Are you sure the park is safe?" Mabel asked.

"Oh, my music keeps the zombies away," said Alphonse. "You do that voodoo," he sang softly as he got into the taxi.

3

Termie
and Extermie

"Mabel, dear, you'll be staying in here," said Mrs. Bamford as she opened the door to Robert's room.

It had taken Robert a long time to get his room exactly the way he wanted it—his collection of monster Halloween masks on the hat rack, his dinosaur stickers from the American Museum of Natural History marching along the molding by his bed, the picture of his father, who lived in Chicago. Mabel wandered around the room, touching everything.

"Robert," said Mrs. Bamford, "I thought you were going to move your stuff into Sam's room."

Robert picked up his Dracula doll, with its one fang missing and one arm missing.

"You're not taking that limbless Dracula doll into my room," Sam said.

Robert glared at his brother. "I'm not leaving him here for *her* to play with," he whispered.

"Oh, how cute," Mabel gushed. She rushed over to the windowsill, where Robert's two gerbils were playing in their cage.

Robert gave her a dirty look. He didn't like his gerbils being called "cute."

"What are their names?" Mabel asked.

"Terminator and Exterminator," said Robert. "I call them Termie and Extermie for short."

Sam pinched his nose. "They smell," he said. "We'll leave 'em here."

"I can't make Termie and Extermie sleep in

the same room as Mabel!" Robert whispered. "They'll have gerbil-mares."

Sam glanced at Mabel. "Bring them along," he said. He grabbed the gerbils' cage. Robert piled as much stuff as he could carry into his arms. Mabel started to unpack.

They had just gotten to Sam's room when they heard Mabel scream.

Robert dropped his Dracula doll. Sam dumped the cage containing the gerbils on the floor. They ran to Robert's room. Mabel was pointing to the window.

"A robber!" she yelled. "Somebody's trying to break in."

Mrs. Bamford came running. "What's wrong?" she asked.

"You're being robbed," Mabel cried. She grabbed Robert's baseball bat. The venetian blind on Robert's window shimmied and shook.

"Mabel, wait!" cried Mrs. Bamford.

A leg covered with jeans snuck through the open part of the window.

Mabel cocked the baseball bat and got ready to bash the robber on the knee.

Robert leaped and snatched the end of the bat.

"What's going on?" asked a boy about fourteen as he poked his head through the window. The boy was carrying a skateboard. "Hi, Mrs. Bamford. Are you guys playing baseball in the house?"

Mabel cowered behind Mrs. Bamford.

"You almost lost a kneecap," said Sam. "This is my cousin Mabel."

"Mabel, this is Willie," said Mrs. Bamford. "He lives upstairs. He sometimes baby-sits for Sam and Robert."

Mabel looked at Willie suspiciously. "Why does he come through the window?"

"The fire escape is faster than the elevator," said Willie. "What smells in here?"

"My present!" exclaimed Mabel. "I forgot all about it."

Mabel ran to one of her orange suitcases. She pulled out a big package. "These are all my favorite foods from San Francisco," said Mabel. "Mom and Dad let me bring them so I wouldn't get homesick. See, there's sourdough bread, and here's the best of all, my favorite cheese. Ta-da! Gorgonzola!"

"Is that what's been stinking?" asked Sam.

Mrs. Bamford took the sourdough bread and the cheese. She held the cheese at arm's length. "It does have rather a strong odor," she said.

"That's what makes it special," said Mabel. "It's made from cow's milk in the Napa Valley. The cows get very tired climbing the hills—and that's what makes the cheese so great."

"I'll put it in the refrigerator," said Mrs. Bamford.

"Say," said Willie, looking around Robert's room. "Where are the gerbils?"

"In my room," said Sam, looking disgusted. The truth was that the tiny rodents made Sam a little nervous. But he would never, never admit it to Robert.

Willie and Mabel followed Sam and Robert into Sam's room.

This time it was Robert's turn to scream. "Oh no," he shouted. The door to the gerbil cage was unhinged. One of the gerbils was happily going around in circles on its wheel, but the other one was nowhere to be seen.

"TERMINATOR!" cried Robert. "He's gone!"

Willie and Sam helped Robert look all over the apartment for Termie. Robert had never realized there were so many places to hide in one apartment.

Mabel followed them, but she didn't seem to be helping much. "Just put out some cheese for him," she said matter-of-factly. "Madeline always comes out for cheese."

"Who's Madeline?" asked Sam.

"My gerbil, " said Mabel. "It's a much nicer name than Terminator or Exterminator. *Madeline* was my favorite book when I was little."

"It's a better name than Mabel," said Sam.

"Well, at least it doesn't rhyme with Spam, Sam-Spam."

"Mabel-label."

Robert ignored them. "What kind of cheese?" he asked.

"Gorgonzola. The cheese that I brought. It's the only cheese that works," Mabel informed Robert.

Robert ran to the refrigerator. He took out the package wrapped in white paper. As he unwrapped it, an incredible odor wafted up and out of his hand.

Sam held his nose.

"That's the most disgusting smell," said Willie.

Robert looked at the cheese. It was a yellow lump with blue veins in it. It looked very old and very rotten.

Mabel sniffed deeply. She smiled. "It reminds me of home," she said.

"Your house must stink," said Sam.

"It's my dad's and my very favorite cheese," said Mabel. "It's a delicacy."

"We'll put it all over the house for Termie," said Robert.

"No you don't! Ma!" screamed Sam.

Mrs. Bamford came hurrying into the kitchen.

"They want to stink up the whole house," complained Sam.

"Let's start in Sam's bedroom," suggested Mabel. "There's where Extermie is, and Termie will want to be back with him."

Robert nodded.

"That stuff is *not* going in my bedroom," yelled Sam.

Mrs. Bamford looked down at the crumbling cheese. "Sam does have a point, Robert."

"If this cheese will get Termie back, it's worth it," said Robert. "He's the one who's important."

"He's just a rodent," said Sam.

"Gerbil," corrected Mabel and Robert together.

Sam glared at them. "A gerbil *is* a rodent," he muttered.

"Why don't you put Extermie back in my room?" Mabel suggested. "I don't mind leaving the cheese in there. Then Termie will find his brother and his cheese."

Robert hesitated. He didn't like Mabel calling *his* room *her* room, but on the other hand, nobody else in his family seemed ready to use the cheese to find Termie.

"Okay," he said.

"Good," said Sam. "I didn't want to sleep with that squeaky wheel even without the cheese."

Robert and Mabel moved the cage back into Robert's room. Robert almost had to close his eyes. Mabel's brightly colored clothes were all over the room.

Mabel unwrapped the package and put the cheese around Robert's bedroom.

Sam stood at the doorway, holding his nose. "This room needs a *real* exterminator," he said.

Mrs. Bamford was holding her nose. "Willie, maybe you can take the kids out to the park. I think everybody could use a little fresh air."

4

Zombie Breath

Mabel changed into a strawberry outfit—that meant strawberry jeans, strawberry socks, a T-shirt with a big strawberry on it, and naturally a strawberry hairband and matching red watchband.

"You look like a jar of Smuckers," said Sam.

"Your cousin's some piece of work," said Willie. "What do you want to show her in the park?"

"Strawberry Fields," said Sam. "Maybe we can plant her there."

They entered the park under a canopy of light-blue wisteria blossoms at 72nd Street. Willie rode his skateboard down the hill. He spun around on the rear two wheels and waved to a bunch of his friends from school. "Hey, Will," shouted one. "What are you doing with that strawberry?"

"Later," shouted Willie. "I'm baby-sitting."

He hopped off his skateboard and put it under his arm.

"I don't like being called a strawberry," said Mabel.

"Then you shouldn't have dressed like one," said Sam.

Willie showed Mabel a beautiful black-and-white mosaic embedded in the ground with the word "Imagine" laid out in tiny stones.

"This part of the park is called Strawberry Fields," Willie explained.

"Oh, I like that name!" gushed Mabel.

"It's dedicated to John Lennon, the Beatle," said Willie, "but it does match your outfit, given that you're dressed like a strawberry."

A group of people hung around the benches surrounding the mosaic, singing "Yellow Submarine," "All You Need Is Love," and other Beatles songs. One woman, with long hair and a patchwork vest, laid flowers on the mosaic.

"I like it here," said Mabel.

"This stuff is boring," said Sam, sidling up to Willie. "Let's go find some zombies." They walked out of Strawberry Fields onto the main drive of the park.

"What zombies?" asked Willie.

"We had this weird taxi driver," Sam explained to Willie. "He said he does voodoo in the park. And he said zombies are dead people who did something wrong and walk the earth."

"I liked that taxi driver," said Robert. "I wish I could find Termie."

"Don't worry, little bro," said Sam.

Robert hated being called little bro.

The sun, setting over the buildings on the West Side of Manhattan, sent shadows across the park.

Mabel grew very quiet. She stuck close to Robert.

Sam and Willie stopped in front of a statue of a falconer, a young boy from the Middle Ages with a hawklike bird on his hand. A breeze blew some old newspapers by the base, making spooky shadows.

Sam pulled Mabel toward him. "Do you see this statue?" he asked.

Mabel nodded.

"The Zombie of Central Park got him. He was once living and breathing like you and me." Sam reached out and tickled Mabel.

She jumped. "You're just trying to scare me."

"No, he's not," said Robert, picking up from his brother. "This park is full of statues that once lived and breathed until the Zombie came, and when he comes again, they live again."

"The Zombie of the park always comes at dusk." Sam cackled.

"Make them stop," Mabel begged Willie.

"They're just telling you the truth," said Willie with a little smile.

"Didn't your own parents tell you that New York was a scary place?" added Sam.

Mabel nodded.

They took Mabel to the statue of Alice in Wonderland. Alice sat on a giant mushroom with the Cheshire Cat grinning from a tree stump by her left hand.

"You can't tell me she was once real," said Mabel, crawling up onto her lap.

"Yes," said Willie solemnly. He pointed to the March Hare and the Mad Hatter. "They all come to life when the Zombie prowls the park."

"What's the Zombie like?" Mabel asked.

"He's got the worst breath in the world— zombie breath," said Sam. "He smells so bad that anything he breathes on instantly gets turned into a statue."

"Zombie breath," repeated Robert.

The shadows in the park got longer and longer. They walked along the drive.

Suddenly Sam grabbed Mabel's arm. "Oh, my gosh. Look over there. A wild animal. Or maybe it's the Zombie! Run. It's ready to pounce!"

Sam started running down the hill with Mabel, holding Mabel's hand. Robert looked up. It was a statue of a mountain lion, perched on a granite cliff. The statue was called Still Hunt, and it has been scaring people for over fifty years.

Robert ran and caught up to the others. Sam grinned at him behind Mabel's back. Sam felt great about getting back at Mabel for calling him Sam-Spam and being an all-around pain in the neck.

But Robert had a funny feeling in the pit of his stomach. He heard a strange drumming in the woods. The shadows of statues seemed to grab out at him, warning him of something. He told himself it was nothing to be scared about. It was just shadows.

Then he remembered that Termie was missing, and the feeling in the pit of his stomach grew.

5

Bad Voodoo in the Air

Mrs. Bamford was waiting for them in the apartment when they got back from the park. "Willie, tomorrow's supposed to be a nice day," she said. "Maybe you could take the kids to the park again."

"She makes us sound like goats," Mabel whispered to Robert.

"Mom, did you find Termie?" Robert interrupted.

Mrs. Bamford shook her head.

The next morning, the entire apartment smelled faintly of very smelly cheese.

"The whole place smells of zombie breath," complained Sam sleepily.

"I think it's just the Gorgonzola," said Mrs. Bamford with a frown. "I should never have agreed to let Mabel scatter it around Robert's room."

The door to Robert's room flew open. The

smell of rotten cheese was quite overpowering.

"Oh," said Mabel. She was wearing a big pink T-shirt with Minnie Mouse on the front. Sam thought she looked a little like a gerbil herself. "I thought maybe Termie was back," she said.

"You mean he didn't come to my room in the night?" Robert asked.

Mabel shook her head. Mrs. Bamford sniffed the air. "Mabel," she said, "we have got to open the windows in this room. I want you to pick up the cheese and throw it down the toilet."

"But Termie is still lost," wailed Robert.

"If that cheese was going to attract him, it would have done so during the night," said Mrs. Bamford. "We're lucky it didn't attract cockroaches."

Robert gave Mabel a dirty look. Now not only was Termie still missing, but his room stank.

"Don't give up, Robert," whispered Mabel. "I'm not going to throw the cheese out." Mabel carefully wrapped up the cheese and put it in her pocket.

Just then Willie arrived via the fire escape.

"Whew," he said, waving his hand in front of his face. "This room stinks."

Mrs. Bamford sighed. "I think maybe you'd better spend the whole day in the park," she said.

Mabel looked suddenly anxious. "Aunt Karen, do you really think the park's safe?"

"Oh, yes," said Mrs. Bamford.

"What about the zombie monsters?" Mabel asked.

"Mabel, you have such an imagination," she said. "The park is very safe. It's like our backyard. Just stick with Willie and Sam and Robert. They know where the dangerous places are." She kissed Sam, Robert, and Mabel good-bye and left for work.

Robert looked very worried. Termie had never been missing all night before.

"Sometimes Madeline gets out into my backyard," said Mabel. "Termie could be there."

"Where?" asked Robert.

"In your backyard, stupid," said Mabel. "Your mother said the park was like your backyard. And even though we're high up, a gerbil might want to feel grass under his feet. I bet he's in the park."

Robert gave Mabel a dirty look. He didn't like being called stupid, and he didn't like the idea of Termie wandering alone in the huge park.

Everybody got dressed. Mabel put on the orange outfit that she had arrived in. Willie took them into the park. Mabel started picking up old pieces of newspaper and looking under them. She looked under the park benches.

"Hey, Mabel," shouted Willie. "Stick with us."

"Let the Zombie get her," muttered Sam.

"Maybe we should give that Zombie business a rest," suggested Willie.

Sam shook his head. "No way. A voodoo zombie with Gorgonzola breath invaded our apartment."

Willie laughed, but Robert didn't.

"Listen," said Robert. They heard the notes of a flute and then the insistent slap of hands on drums. The rhythm of the drums kept changing as it followed the flute on its flights of fancy. It was very strange music, but somehow it sounded right. They followed the beat of the drums.

"It's zombie voodoo music," Sam whispered in Mabel's ear.

A large crowd had gathered, and Mabel, Sam, and Robert couldn't see the musicians over the heads of the people.

The group finished their piece to great applause. Some of the crowd started to move away. Others dropped coins and dollar bills into the flute case.

"Look!" said Sam. "It's Adolph."

"Alphonse," corrected Mabel.

The taxi driver looked up when he heard his name. His hands were resting on his large conga drums.

"Hi," said Sam. "Remember us? We were in your taxi yesterday."

"*Mais oui,*" said Alphonse. "But yes."

"Your music is great," said Robert.

"Awesome," agreed Willie.

Alphonse smiled. He gave Robert a piercing look. "You look sad," he said.

Robert didn't know it showed. "My gerbil is lost," he said.

"I'm sorry," said Alphonse.

"Do you think you could do some voodoo and bring him back?" Robert asked seriously.

"It'll work better than Gorgonzola," Sam said, snickering.

Mabel interrupted. "You don't need voodoo.

I've got a plan to get him back," she said. She took out the package of stale Gorgonzola and started to sprinkle it around the tree.

Alphonse's music partner, the flutist, got angry. "Hey, little girl. I don't like people littering my park."

"I'm not littering," said Mabel. "This is biodegradable, and I am helping Robert find Termie."

"Mabel," said Willie with a sigh, "you can't stink up the park the way you did the Bamfords' apartment."

"Besides," said Sam, "Mom told you to throw that out."

"I am," said Mabel. "But what if Termie got out into the park? He has to be hungry. He'll smell the Gorgonzola and come back."

"I don't like litterers," said the flute player. He kicked at an old piece of newspaper that was swirling by his feet.

"Malcolm, calm down," said Alphonse. "This is Malcolm Mason. He's a great flutist, but he's got a temper."

Malcolm and Alphonse started to put their instruments away. Malcolm's flute needed just a little case, but Alphonse had a huge carrying suitcase with wheels on it for his congas.

"Let's go play by Balto," said Alphonse to Malcolm, trying to calm him down. "That's always a good place to attract crowds."

"What's Balto?" asked Mabel.

"Oh, just one of the Zombie's victims," said Sam, winking at Willie.

"What is this zombie?" asked Alphonse. "Balto's a statue of a dog."

"Right," said Sam. "He was a real dog. Until the Gorgonzola Zombie turned him into bronze. That's what the Zombie does. All these statues were once alive, but with one puff of Gorgonzola breath the Zombie turned them to stone—just like that." Sam snapped his fingers.

Alphonse shook his head. "You shouldn't joke about zombies," he said. He finished packing up his drums and started to head away with Malcolm.

"Yeah," said Sam. "Now that Mabel's in town, soon the whole city will stink like Gorgonzola breath."

Mabel shivered.

"It could happen," said Sam.

Robert wished that Sam would stop teasing Mabel.

Robert ran after Alphonse. "You never told

me if voodoo would help get my gerbil back."

"It depends on the spirits," said Alphonse. He sniffed. "There is bad voodoo in the air."

"I think that's just Mabel's Gorgonzola," said Robert seriously. "But do you mean it's like you said in the taxi? If I did something bad, it could come back to haunt me?"

Alphonse nodded.

Robert shivered. Maybe losing Termie was punishment for scaring Mabel. Stranger things had happened. Bad voodoo.

6

A Scared and Lonely Little Girl

"Robert, face it. Termie's gone," said Sam the next morning as Robert moped around the house. "He's gone to the giant squeaky wheel in the sky."

Robert bit his lip. He was reading a book called *All About Voodoo* that he had found in the library.

"That was mean," said Mabel. "I'd be nicer if I was the one who left Termie's cage door open."

"We should have let the Gorgonzola Zombie in the park eat you," said Sam.

"If it's going to eat anybody, it will be you," said Mabel. She ran into Robert's room and slammed the door.

"Sam and Robert," warned Mrs. Bamford. "I want you to start behaving nicely to your cousin and stop teasing her. It's not funny."

"All I'm doing is reading a book," complained Robert.

"Mom, she really is a little monster," said Sam. "She got off the plane and called my nose a honker."

"Well, I used to tease her dad, my brother, about his big nose. Maybe she's homesick for her mom and dad."

"Zombies don't get homesick," said Sam.

Robert put his book down. He thought about the first time Sam and he had teased Mabel and got her thinking she was his younger cousin. Bad things had started happening right after. "Mom, do you think Termie is dead?" he asked his mother anxiously.

Mrs. Bamford put her arms around Robert. "I don't know, honey. I hope not," she said. "Maybe he'll show up by tomorrow."

But the next morning Termie was still missing.

Sam and Robert woke up in lousy moods. Robert was sure that he would never see Termie again. And Sam *did* feel a little guilty that he had been the one to drop Termie. Sam hated feeling guilty.

Late in the day Willie popped down the fire escape to see if Termie had been found.

"We think Termie's deader than a zombie," said Sam.

"Did you find his body?" Willie asked.

"No, that's why he's a zombie," teased Sam. When Sam was upset, he tended to make sick jokes.

Willie looked thoughtful. "Mrs. Bamford, do you want me to take the kids to the park today?"

"Please," begged Mrs. Bamford. "They've been moping inside all morning."

"Maybe we'll go roller-skating," suggested Willie.

"I'm a very good roller skater," said Mabel, perking up.

"I bet," said Willie. Mabel went into Robert's room and came out in purple-and-black bicycle pants and a purple top.

"Are you a grape today?" asked Sam.

Mabel stuck her lower lip out. She looked like she wanted to cry. "This is my mother's favorite outfit," she said. "She's got one to match."

"Your mother dresses like a grape too?" teased Sam.

"Sam Bamford, I hate you!" screamed Mabel.

"Calm down, Mabel," said Willie. "A skate in the park will cool everybody out."

They went outside. Ray McKenna, the super, was standing in front of the building with his giant broom. The wind had picked up, and some loose pieces of garbage were sent swirling down the street. Ray chased after the garbage, muttering to himself. Mabel watched him go.

They rented skates and took them to the park. Willie helped Mabel put hers on. "Be careful," he warned. "The park is full of hills and . . ." Willie didn't get a chance to finish his sentence. Mabel was off the park bench and flying down the pathway, gracefully looping and turning. "I should have guessed," said Willie.

Sam and Robert looked at each other. Neither of them was half as good as Mabel. "I wish there really was a Gorgonzola Zombie," muttered Sam. "I'd like him to turn her into a statue, skates and all."

"She's not that bad," said Robert.

Sam stared at him.

"Well, at least she didn't call Termie a zombie," said Robert. "Wait up, Mabel," he shouted.

But Mabel had disappeared down the hill.

"Mabel!" yelled Willie. He took off after her, but he caught his wheel on a crack in the pavement. Willie went sprawling. Willie was much better on a skate*board* then he was on roller skates.

"Are you okay?" asked Sam.

"Go find Mabel," said Willie breathlessly, picking himself up and looking at the scrape on his arm.

Sam and Robert awkwardly skated down the hill.

"Mabel! Mabel!" they shouted.

Willie caught up with them.

"Did you find her?" he asked. He sounded nervous.

The park was full of people. "I wish she had worn her strawberry outfit," said Robert. "There are a lot of people wearing purple."

"Purple and black kind of look like shadows," said Sam.

Willie searched the entire area. He couldn't find Mabel anywhere.

"Where is she?" asked Robert, sounding worried.

"Maybe the Zombie got her," said Sam.

"This isn't funny," said Robert. "She's lost, and doesn't know the park the way we do."

"Maybe we'd better find a cop," said Willie.

"There's one," said Robert, pointing down the hill toward the statue of the falconer, where a huge crowd had gathered.

Sam skidded to a stop. He had never learned to stop very well. When they got to the statue, people were pointing up to it and holding their noses.

"What's going on?" asked Sam.

"Someone smeared something all over the statues," said a stranger. "They all stink today."

Sam looked up at the statue. It had something smeared around its mouth and around the mouth of the falcon.

"It's a crime," said the stranger.

"Have you seen a little girl dressed in purple?" Robert asked. The stranger shook his head.

"She looks like a purple zombie," said Sam.

Robert punched him on the arm.

Willie went up to talk to the officer. He pointed up to the statue. Willie skated back to Sam and Robert. He was out of breath.

"What did he say?" Sam asked.

"The police have their hands full today," said Willie. "The cop said somebody's been doing something to the statues. He said if we don't find Mabel in a half hour to report it to the precinct. I'm really worried. Your mom's going to kill me."

"Maybe Mabel went to the statue of Alice in Wonderland?" suggested Robert. "At least it's someplace she knows."

They skated over to the statue of Alice in Wonderland. For once there were no children clambering up Alice's skirt. Instead everybody was staying a good distance away. A park ranger was climbing over the Mad Hatter toward Alice's mouth.

Another ranger kept the crowd away.

"Whatever it is," said a ranger who was cleaning the mouth, "it really stinks." She took out a cloth and tried to wipe up some of the goo.

"Have you seen a little girl dressed in purple and black on roller skates?"

"I haven't had time to look at anything," said the ranger. "I'd like to catch the monster who smeared cheese all over the statues!"

"Cheese!" exclaimed Sam.

"The Gorgonzola Zombie," whispered Robert.

The ranger laughed. "Very funny, little boy." Then she looked at Robert suspiciously. "How did you know it was Gorgonzola?"

"Come on, Robert," said Sam, grabbing his brother. The ranger watched them carefully.

"Gorgonzola Zombie—Mabel's missing," hissed Robert. "What if the Zombie's got her?"

"Get ahold of yourself, little bro," said Sam, smiling at the ranger. "Sorry we bothered you."

Willie skated up to them. "I don't see her anywhere," he said, sounding really worried. "If we don't find her in a few minutes, I'm going to the precinct house."

"Listen," said Robert. They heard the haunting beat of a drum. The sun had begun to set over the West Side, and the shadows were getting longer. The drums reminded Robert of the first night they had brought Mabel to the park—the night Termie had disappeared.

"The Zombie's got her for sure," said Robert, shaking his head from side to side. He sank down on a bench. "First it got Termie. Then it got Mabel. Now it's smearing cheese all over the statues. Soon it'll cover the whole city."

"My brother's losing it," said Sam to Willie.

"We've got to find Mabel," said Willie. The sound of the drums got louder and louder.

Robert got off the park bench. Slowly, almost as if he were in a trance, he followed the drumbeats.

"Robert!" yelled Willie. "We've got to stick

together until we find Mabel!"

Robert didn't turn his head. He followed the sound of the drums.

Sam and Willie stared at each other. Willie took Sam's hand and skated after Robert.

Robert skated down a path, past the statue of Alice in Wonderland. There in a glade were Alphonse and Malcolm. In front of them Mabel was skating, doing figure eights in time to the music.

For a moment it was as if the noises of the city had disappeared. There was only the beat of the conga drums and the melody of the flute and Mabel dipping and swooping on her skates.

Then Willie broke the spell. He grabbed Mabel and shook her. "Mabel! We've been looking all over for you. Never go off by yourself! You scared me out of my wits."

Mabel started to cry.

Alphonse stopped drumming. "She got lost in the crowd by the statues," he said. "She found us, and we knew that you would hear our music and find her."

Robert stared at him. He seemed to come out of his trance.

"How did you know?" Robert asked.

"We knew," said Alphonse. "Mabel, stop your crying."

"Yeah, crybaby. We were the ones who had to look for you. You had Willie about to call the police," said Sam angrily.

"Don't yell at her," warned Alphonse. "She is a scared and lonely little girl, far from home."

"You don't know her," muttered Sam.

Willie took a deep breath. "Mabel, don't ever leave my side again when we're in the park," he repeated. "You stick close to me."

Robert was staring at Alphonse. "Did you hear about what's been happening to the statues in the park?" he asked.

Alphonse nodded as he packed up his drums. "Our work is done here . . . for today."

"Is it voodoo?" Robert asked seriously. "Is that how you found Mabel and we found you? Is that what's happening?"

Alphonse raised an eyebrow, but he didn't answer.

"Good voodoo or bad voodoo?" Robert whispered half to himself.

Alphonse patted Robert on the back. He and the flute player disappeared into the trees.

7

We're Not Crybabies

"Sam! Robert! Mabel!" shrieked Mrs. Bamford.

Sam and Robert rolled out of bed sleepily. "Did you find Termie?" asked Robert.

"No," admitted Mrs. Bamford. "But wait until you see the papers." Mrs. Bamford was sitting at the breakfast table with all the Saturday newspapers around her the way she always did on a weekend. Mrs. Bamford loved newspapers, and she needed to read them for her job as a television news producer.

"N.Y. STATUES HAVE BAD BREATH!" read one.

Another read "IS PARK GETTING CHEESY?"

Mrs. Bamford read aloud from one of the papers.

"A mysterious affliction hit many of the park statues overnight. The statues gave out a peculiar odor that seemed to come from a smelly substance. The police have yet to analyze the substance in the labs officially. However, our restaurant correspondent on the scene reports that the substance is definitely Gorgonzola cheese. Who is responsible and why? Detectives are looking into this bizarre occurrence."

Mrs. Bamford looked at Sam, Robert, and Mabel. "Gorgonzola? You children didn't have anything to do with this, did you?"

"Ma," protested Sam. "We're no zombies."

Mrs. Bamford put down the paper. "What's that noise?" she asked. "I hear scratching!"

"Termie!" cried Robert. "It must be Termie."

Robert looked under the pile of newspapers.

"The noise is coming from Robert's room," said Mrs. Bamford, rising from the kitchen table.

"It's got to be Termie," said Mabel. "I told you he'd come back."

Mabel rushed into Robert's room. The

scratching noise was louder.

Extermie got extremely agitated in his cage, scurrying under the shredded newspapers at the bottom of his cage.

"Oh, Termie, come back to me!" wailed Robert, picking up Mabel's clothes and looking under them.

"This room looks like a fruit stand," said Sam, staring at Mabel's varicolored clothes strewn over every available surface.

Mrs. Bamford picked up different pieces of clothing. "Mabel, you really do have to clean up this room."

"Mom, Termie's scratching! I can hear him!" said Robert excitedly.

Mrs. Bamford lifted the venetian blind.

Willie's face was plastered against the top window.

"Willie," said Mrs. Bamford, opening the glass window and then the screen. "You gave me a fright."

"So did you," said Willie. "The window and screen were locked! It's never locked. I've been scratching and knocking for what seems like hours."

"I locked it so the Zombie wouldn't get me," said Mabel.

Robert sank down on his bed with his head in his hand. "I'll never see Termie again," he wailed. He started to sniffle.

Mrs. Bamford patted him on the back.

"Did you all read about the park?" asked Willie.

"It's very peculiar," said Mrs. Bamford.

Suddenly Mabel sat down on the bed next to Robert and started to sob.

Robert wiped his eyes.

"What's she crying about?" demanded Sam.

"I miss Termie too," sniffled Mabel.

"He's not your gerbil. He's mine," said Robert.

"I know what it's like to be far from home and alone," wailed Mabel.

Mrs. Bamford gathered Mabel under one arm and Robert under the other.

Sam and Willie looked at them. Sam sighed. "I hate crybabies," said Sam.

Robert and Mabel dried their eyes. They glared at Sam.

"We're not crybabies," they said in unison.

Mrs. Bamford stood up. "I think it's time I see for myself what's going on in the park," she said. "Get dressed; we'll all go."

8

A Cousin Made of Gorgonzola

The rangers had set up barricades around the statues. People were standing around in small groups, pointing to the statues and shaking their heads.

Mrs. Bamford went up to one of the rangers and started asking questions. Robert felt guilty. "It's like the Gorgonzola Zombie is growing," he whispered to Sam. "First, I lost Termie because we tried to scare Mabel. Now, the whole city is suffering."

"Robert," warned Sam. "You're going around the bend here. I think there's a sane reason for everything."

"Oh yeah?" asked Robert. "Name one."

"Willie," whispered Sam, glancing over his shoulder at Willie, who was walking with Mabel.

Willie stopped to talk to one of his buddies.

"He got the idea from the stink in our house. He and his pals could be the Gorgonzola Zombie. It could all be a joke."

Robert looked back at Willie. "Do you really think he could have done all this?"

"He's got lots of friends," suggested Sam. "It makes more sense than your voodoo theory."

Mabel left Willie's side and came running up to them. "What are you two whispering about?" she demanded.

"Don't tell her," Sam said quickly.

"She's our cousin," said Robert. "If the Zombie is . . ." Robert paused. "You know who . . . we should warn her."

"Who?" whispered Mabel.

Robert cocked his head at Willie.

"Willie!" shouted Mabel. Sam slapped his hand over Mabel's mouth.

Mabel squirmed. She bit Sam's hand. "Ouch!" Sam exclaimed. "You're worse than a gerbil."

"Willie's the Living Dead?" exclaimed Mabel.

Willie came running up to them. "What's going on?" he asked.

"Nothing," said Mabel and Sam in unison.

Robert was staring at the ground.

Willie looked annoyed. "Well, play nicely," he warned. "Your mom asked me to look after you. She wants to talk to another ranger. I'll just be right over here with my friends. And I won't let you out of sight, any of you."

"Yeah, the Gorgonzola-breath friends," said Sam as soon as Willie turned his back on them.

"I know it isn't Willie," said Robert. "I think it's got to be something stranger than that."

"I agree with Robert," said Mabel. "I think the Gorgonzola Zombie is real. Didn't Alphonse say that zombies make life miserable for people?"

"My life has been miserable," said Robert.

"Exactly," said Mabel.

Mabel stopped short. She grabbed Robert's arm and squeezed it.

"Ouch!" cried Robert. Mabel couldn't talk. She was staring down at the ground and pointing.

"What now?" demanded Sam.

Robert's mouth dropped open. He pointed down at the ground too.

"Look, it's footprints," gasped Robert.

"Zombies don't leave footprints," said Sam.

"These are weird," said Robert. He and Mabel pointed to two round impressions on the soft ground. The circles were close together, and they didn't look like any kind of human or animal prints.

"Give me a break," said Sam.

"No," said Robert. "Look at this, Sam. It's very strange. What else could it be? Should we show it to the rangers? Get Mom."

"Right," said Sam. "The rangers are really going to believe you when you tell them it's the Zombie's footsteps."

Mabel and Robert stared at each other. Sam

wandered away to sit on a rock. He could see Willie and his friends, talking and looking over at them.

"Those guys over there are your zombies," said Sam. "They're laughing their heads off at you because you believe them."

"Yeah?" said Robert. "Prove it."

Sam started wandering around. "Now look," he said. "Here's a clue."

Sam pointed to two wheeled tracks in the dirt. "If those weren't made by a skateboard, my name's not Sam Bamford."

"There are thousands of skateboards in the park," argued Robert. "Why would those be Willie's?"

"Because it makes more sense than your voodoo theory."

Willie came down from the hill with his friends. "What are you kids doing?" he asked.

"Nothing much." Sam shrugged.

Willie looked down at the tracks in the dirt. "Let's go," he said.

Sam looked at him. "You know, Willie, we're your friends. We've known you all our lives. You can trust us."

Willie stared at Sam. "Thanks," he muttered.

Sam persisted. "Isn't there something you want to tell us?"

"No," said Willie.

"It's okay," Sam mouthed to Willie, making his lips make the letters O.K. "We would never tell on you." Sam gave Mabel a serious look. "Even Mabel."

Willie just shook his head. He bent down and ruffled Sam's hair. Sam hated to have his hair ruffled. "Right, little man."

Sam disliked being called little man almost as much as Robert disliked being called little bro.

"Willie, all jokes aside," said Sam. "It's time to tell these two kids what's really going on."

Willie scrunched up his face. "Sam, is your elevator stopping on the top floor?" he asked.

Sam laughed as if he and Willie were sharing a joke. Sam just knew that it was Willie himself who had done it, not some voodoo zombie spirit.

Mabel held on to Willie's hand as they walked out of the park.

"Do you realize that everything Mabel touches starts to smell like Gorgonzola?" Sam pointed out to Robert.

"Maybe she's the Gorgonzola Zombie,"

whispered Robert.

"A cousin made out of Gorgonzola. Weirder things have happened," said Sam.

"I don't think so," said Robert.

9

A Good Zombie?

The next morning there was a knock on the front door. "I wonder who that is," said Mrs. Bamford, looking up from the newspapers. It was Willie and his parents, David and Sukey Rosenbaum.

"It's nice to see you off the fire escape," said Mrs. Bamford to Willie.

"Are you coming to the rally to clean up the park?" asked Mrs. Rosenbaum. "The mayor is saying that we've got to get together and clean up the park ourselves."

Sam went up to Willie. "Are you going to this rally?" he asked.

"I wouldn't miss it," said Willie.

Sam winked at him.

"Sam, do you have something in your eye?" Willie asked.

"Come on, kids," said Mrs. Bamford. "Let's go with the Rosenbaums."

Mabel looked worried. She wondered if the

Gorgonzola Zombie was taking over the city. Mrs. Bamford took her hand. "Oh, don't worry, Mabel," she said. "I've been to lots of rallies and protests in Central Park, but never one *for* the park. Sukey is right. If we don't do something to clean up our own backyard, who will?"

As they got downstairs Ray McKenna was putting up a sign in the lobby: GONE TO RALLY! SO SHOULD YOU!

"Finally, somebody's done something to wake people up to the need to clean up this city," said Ray. He got his big broom and rushed toward the park.

"Maybe Ray is the Gorgonzola Zombie," whispered Mabel. "Maybe he's a good zombie and he wants people to clean up the park."

"It's Willie, I tell you," whispered Sam.

Robert didn't say anything.

It was a cloudless summer day in the city. The leaves on the trees shimmered slightly in the breeze. Men in suits, women in dresses, teenagers on skateboards, bicyclists in skin-tight Lycra, all headed into the park.

As the Bamfords and the Rosenbaums entered the park, a volunteer offered them buckets of water and wet rags.

"What's this for?" Sam asked.

"We're asking everybody to clean up the park today," said the volunteer. "That's the point of the rally. Everyone is getting a bucket and rag. If everybody here just takes five minutes to wash something and to pick up the trash and to remember to do it every day, the park will be clean."

Sam took a bucket and rag. Mrs. Bamford and the Rosenbaums each took a bucket.

"This can't be New York," said Mrs. Bamford as she looked around at people smiling at each other, picking up trash, and cleaning off the benches and statues.

"Oh, it's New York at it's best," said Sukey Rosenbaum with a smile.

"The Gorgonzola Zombie is responsible for all this," whispered Mabel in an awed voice. "Maybe he always was a good zombie."

Sam gave her a disgusted look. "A good zombie. It was you, Willie, wasn't it?"

"What was you, Willie?" asked Mrs. Bamford.

Willie shook his head. "Nothing. You know—these little kids like to make up stuff."

Sam stuck out his lower lip. He hated being lumped with Mabel and Robert and called a little kid. He hated that even more than being called a little man.

Mrs. Bamford and the Rosenbaums went to clean up the statue of William Shakespeare.

Mabel, Sam, and Robert were left alone with Willie.

Sam had had just about all he could take. He grabbed Willie by the arm and shoved him up against a tree.

"All right," he warned. "Are you telling me—no lies—that you aren't the Zombie?"

"Sam," warned Robert.

"I want to know the truth," demanded Sam.

Willie pushed Sam's arm away. "You kids are all nuts," he said. He was mad.

He stalked away.

Mrs. Bamford came up to them. "What's wrong with Willie?" she asked.

"Nothing," said Sam through gritted teeth.

"Why don't you go over to Balto and start to clean him up," said Mrs. Bamford. "I'll be right there. I want to talk to some more rangers."

Mabel, Sam, and Robert trudged over the

hill to the statue of the dog.

A flock of pigeons flew into the air, startling them. The pigeons' wings made an eerie noise as they flapped by. Mabel grabbed Robert's arm as a pigeon flew past her.

"There's zombies everywhere today," she whispered.

Robert swallowed. "You're right," he whispered. Sam stayed close to the two of them.

When they got to Balto, Robert had to pinch his nose. "Wow, talk about dog breath," he said.

Sam took out his rag, dipped it into the water, and started to clean off the statue.

"I don't get it," said Mabel. "Was Willie really the Gorgonzola Zombie?"

Sam shrugged. He dipped his rag into the bucket and started to wipe off the base of the snout.

"I think it's all just a bad dream," said Sam.

"Bad dreams don't smell like this one," said Robert, wiping some of the dried Gorgonzola off the dog's snout.

Mabel helped him. "It's real Gorgonzola," she said, sniffing. "It's not a dream."

Once again a flock of pigeons took off,

beating their wings in the air.

Mabel stood at the base of the statue and stared at the pigeons. Then she gazed into the woods.

"What?" demanded Sam.

"Shh," said Mabel.

She slipped off the base of the statue and started to tiptoe into the woods.

"Mabel!" warned Sam. "Don't get lost again."

"Listen," whispered Mabel.

Robert and Sam cupped their hands to their ears. They heard drumming.

Robert slid off the statue and followed Mabel into the woods. Mabel took Robert's hand. They tiptoed toward the sound. Sam threw down his rag and caught up to them. He took Mabel's other hand.

"You aren't going anywhere without me," he said. "You'll get lost again."

"The drumming," whispered Mabel. "It's the Zombie."

"It's not the Zombie," scoffed Sam. "It's Alphonse."

Mabel and Robert looked at each other. A squirrel scurried by their feet.

As they got deeper into the woods, they found Alphonse, leaning against a tree with his conga drums. "Are you kids doing a good job of cleaning the statues?" he asked.

Robert, Mabel, and Sam nodded.

"Good," said Alphonse. "I just wanted to be sure." He started to pack his conga drums into their carrying case.

Mabel ran to where he had been standing and pointed to the ground. There were the same round impressions that she had seen by the statues.

"Alphonse?" she whispered.

Alphonse turned around. Sam and Robert stared from the impression on the ground to Alphonse and back again.

Then Sam saw the tracks of the wheels of the drum's carrying case. "You're the Gorgonzola Zombie," said Sam.

Alphonse put a finger to his lips. "You and your little cousin gave me the idea. We had to do something to wake people up," he said.

"Wake them from the dead," whispered Robert. "That's what you were doing."

"People were dead to how beautiful their park is. Cheese didn't hurt the statues. It

washes right off."

"I still don't get it," said Mabel. "Are you telling me that you *are* the Gorgonzola Zombie?"

Alphonse just smiled. "Let's just say I'm his instrument," he said, patting his drum case.

"I never did find Termie," said Robert sadly. "I guess nobody can bring him back from the dead."

"Not from the dead," agreed Alphonse.

Mabel paused. She closed her eyes.

"What are you doing?" Sam asked annoyed.

"I'm making a wish," said Mabel. "Now that I know the Gorgonzola Zombie isn't all bad, I'm asking him to help find Termie."

"You are crazy," said Sam.

Alphonse ignored Sam. "When you finish cleaning Balto, you'll be going home," he said to Robert. "Home is where the heart is. My heart has always been in the park."

"My home is far away," said Mabel. She sounded sad.

"I know," said Alphonse. "But look to your heart," he said with a knowing expression.

Alphonse dragged his case away.

"He's not a zombie," said Sam.

"What do you think he meant when he said 'look to your heart' to me?" asked Mabel.

"Maybe he wanted to know if you had one," said Sam.

"Lay off," said Robert. Mabel was looking very sad and very homesick.

10

A Squeak of Joy

"What a wonderful day!" Mrs. Bamford exclaimed to the superintendent as they got into the elevator.

"Look at the sidewalk. Not a piece of trash on it," said Ray. "It's a miracle."

They rode up in the elevator. Mrs. Bamford put her key in the lock. "I'm exhausted," she said. She looked around. The apartment was a mess, with newspapers and the kids' games and books all over the place.

"Now that we've cleaned up the park, maybe we should clean up the apartment," she suggested.

She glanced into Robert's room. Mabel's brightly colored clothes were still strewn all over the place.

"My room looks like Miss Piggy slept in it," complained Robert.

"Mabel," said Mrs. Bamford, "I'd like you to clean this up."

Mabel made a face. She dragged her feet toward Robert's room. Then she stopped halfway through the door. "What's that?" she exclaimed. "Sam, Robert! Come here!"

"We're not helping you clean this room," said Sam.

"I heard a sound," said Mabel. She started picking up her clothes from the floor: A purple skirt, a raspberry pair of tights, a banana-yellow T-shirt, all got flung on the bed.

Then Robert picked up a sweatshirt with a strawberry-red heart on it. A sandy, furry face appeared under the folds of the sweatshirt.

"Termie!" shrieked Robert, scooping up the little rodent.

From his cage on the windowsill, Extermie gave a squeak. "That's a squeak of joy," said Mabel. "He's so happy to see his friend."

"How can you tell it's a squeak of joy?" asked Sam. "Maybe he doesn't like having to share his space."

"It's a squeak of joy," said Robert. "He doesn't mind sharing with someone he likes."

"Oh, brother," said Sam with a sigh.

"Oh, cousin," said Mabel.

"She *is* our cousin," said Robert.

"I know why Alphonse said home is where the heart is," said Mabel, folding up her sweatshirt with the heart on it. "He knows what it's like to miss your home."

"You could call your parents if you're homesick," suggested Robert. "It's only three hours' difference to San Francisco."

Mabel stared at him. "You know, my parents haven't gotten younger since I've been away," she said thoughtfully. "My dad is still your mom's older brother."

Robert looked a little sheepish. He put his hand in the cage and patted Termie. "We made that up."

"Just like we made up the Gorgonzola Zombie," said Sam.

Mabel and Robert looked at each other and then at Termie.

"I'm not sure we *did* make that up," said Robert.

Through the open window, overlooking the park, Sam, Robert, and Mabel were sure they could hear the haunting sound of flute and drums.

"The Gorgonzola Zombie's out there," said Robert.

"He knew where Termie was," said Mabel.

"He knows all," said Sam with a sigh, realizing that the Gorgonzola Zombie was here to stay.